"It's going to be a spelling *bee*," Mr. Bishop explained. "Everyone will take their turn, standing here in front of the class, spelling their word out loud."

B felt her stomach flutter. Oh, she wanted those tickets! But how could she stand in front of the class and spell well enough to win?

She could stay up late every night studying. But standing up in front of others — well, there was nothing that could prepare her for that horror.

B clenched her fists. If only she had her magic and could work a spell to eliminate stage fright.

But she couldn't.

She'd have to earn those tickets the hard way.

As usual.

DISCOVER ALL THE MAGIC!

Spelling B and the Missing Magic
Spelling B and the Trouble with Secrets
Spelling B and the Runaway Spell

Spelling B

And the Missing Magic

By Lexi Connor

SCHOLASTIC INC.

New York   Toronto   London   Auckland   Sydney
Mexico City   New Delhi   Hong Kong   Buenos Aires

ISBN-13: 978-0-545-11736-4
ISBN-10: 0-545-11736-4

Series created by Working Partners Ltd.

12 11 10 9 8 7 6 5 4 3   9 10 11 12 13 14/0

Printed in the U.S.A.
First printing, September 2009

Special thanks to Julie Berry

To Daniel

Chapter 1

"Beeeee-atrix," B's mother called up the stairs. "Breakfast!"

B cinched her ponytail and took one last look in the bathroom mirror. "Maybe today," she told her reflection. Then she plucked a little pot of her sister's lip balm from the medicine cabinet and chanted softly:

"Let this be my first spell in rhyme:
Cherry lip gloss, change to lime!"

She squeezed her eyes tight, then opened them. Nothing had happened. She sniffed to make sure. It was still cherry. Just like yesterday, and every day since her eleventh birthday, more than three months ago.

Her cat, Nightshade, twined himself between her ankles and meowed.

"I *know* it didn't work," she told him. "Don't remind me."

He purred in answer. He probably didn't understand her, but with Nightshade, B could never be sure.

B grabbed her backpack from her bedroom and stuffed her battered copy of *Through the Looking Glass* inside. She hurried down the stairs, two at a time, and slid into her chair, the last one at the breakfast table.

"Dawn, please," B's mom said to B's older sister. "No mascara at breakfast."

Dawn sighed and shoved her makeup back into her purse, muttering:

"Dawn is quick, her rhymes are cunning.
Dawn's dark lashes are thick and stunning!"

And, poof! She looked like she'd just had a makeover.

B rolled her eyes. Her sister's spells were *so* superficial.

Dawn made a face. "What's the matter, B? Jealous?"

"Girls, girls," their mother scolded. "No time for bickering. The bus will be here soon." She pointed toward the table and said, in a singsongy voice:

"Butter melt and batter bubble,

Golden pancakes! On the double!"

And fragrant stacks of steaming pancakes, drenched in syrup and butter, appeared on everyone's plates.

B's dad rubbed the sleep out of his eyes, mumbling:

"Roast it, grind it, brew it up.

Coffee, black, in my favorite cup."

The coffee machine on the counter whirred and hissed, then beeped. A full pot detached itself and floated over to the table. It dipped low over Dad's summer solstice celebration mug, filling it without spilling a drop. It then paused by Mom's cup, but she shook her head. "No, thank you. I'm cutting back."

Dawn frowned at her plate and said:

"Lighter, please. Fewer calories.

A syrup smile is all Dawn needs."

That's not even a perfect rhyme, B thought, *but it doesn't matter*. Dawn's pat of butter and half her syrup vanished, leaving a happy face made of syrup on her top pancake. She grinned and flicked her long blond hair behind her back before digging in.

It was so unfair. Everything Dawn did came out perfectly.

B's annoyance faded when she tasted her pancakes. Mom's breakfast spells were the best. She'd won first prize at the Witchin' Kitchen Competition for her dandelion donuts, three years straight, with a second place prize for her famous eel soup.

"Great pancakes, Mom," B said. "Will you pass the apple juice, please?"

Her family lowered their forks and studied her. B felt her face turn red. She should have just gotten some milk from the fridge, instead of drawing attention to the fact that she still couldn't perform spells.

Mom's kind face was full of concern. "Try it,

dear," she said. "Just a little juice-summoning rhyme. Who knows? This might be the day!"

But of course B already knew that it wasn't. While her family and all their witching friends could rhyme their way out of stomachaches, traffic jams, and washing dishes, B was left doing things the hard way.

B sighed. She'd have to try. It didn't help, her family waiting and watching like that. Performing in front of crowds, even just her three family members, made B extremely nervous. She tried to think. What rhymed with juice? Loose, goose, hangman's noose. Arg. Her family made this rhyming business seem so easy.

Well, she thought, *here goes nothing*. She closed her eyes and recited:

"Syrup sweeter than chocolate mousse
Makes me want some apple juice!"

B opened her eyes again. Her glass was still empty, and the juice carton hadn't budged. Her parents' hopeful expressions froze and Dawn went back to eating her magically cheery pancakes.

Her mom poured B some apple juice by hand. B was grateful she didn't use magic.

"That was a lovely rhyme," she said, smiling sweetly at B. "Rhyming 'mousse' with 'juice.' How original!"

"Yes, nice touch with the chocolate part," B's dad said, ruffling B's bangs. He worked as a senior marketing manager at Enchanted Chocolates Worldwide. "Which reminds me . . ." He flipped out his portable Crystal Ballphone. "Marcus! Hey, this is Felix. Can you conjure up sales figures for last quarter in our mousse and pudding sector?"

Her parents' efforts to cheer her up only made it worse. B poked at her pancakes with her fork. She wasn't hungry anymore.

"I just remembered something I need for school," she said, tossing down her napkin. "Can I be excused?"

Her mother nodded. B ran back upstairs. In her room she reached under her mattress and pulled out the rhyming dictionary she'd bought with her birthday money from Granny Grogg. She hid it in her backpack, then slid down the banister and out the front door just as the bus stopped at the end of the street.

"Bye, girls," her mom called as Dawn and B ran to the bus. "Have a charmed day!"

Chapter 2

B braced herself, expecting Dawn to say something about her magic before they got on the bus, but her older sister didn't say a word. She just hurried to the back to sit with her high school friends. B searched around for her best friend, George, but he hadn't made it in time. For a kid who won the 50-meter dash last year on track and field day, George sure moved slowly in the mornings. B took an empty seat near the front, where she could practice rhyming without anyone seeing.

"H . . . I . . . J . . . juice," she said under her breath. "Here it is." She scanned up and down for interesting words. "Chartreuse? Mongoose. Obtuse.

Sluice? *Huh?* Truce. I'm going to need a regular dictionary to look these up."

None of the words worked any better than "mousse." B flicked through the book, checking for words that rhymed with "drink" and "glass." Nothing exciting there, either. *Pass a glass? Fink, stink, juice to drink . . .* hopeless.

B didn't know if it was her rhymes that didn't work or if it was just her — the only eleven-year-old witch in the whole Magical Rhyming Society that didn't have her powers.

The bus stopped at the high school. Dawn and her friends made their way down the aisle. Just then Jason Jameson popped up in the seat in front of B and grabbed her book.

"Hey, everybody, look at this!" he yelled. "*Hornet* reads the dictionary!"

The sight of Jason's freckle-plastered face leering down at her, plus yet another of his awful bee-related nicknames, was enough to ruin even the happiest day. And this wasn't one of those days.

Dawn shot out her softball fast-pitch arm and snagged the rhyming dictionary out of Jason's hands. "You should try reading the dictionary some-time," she said, glaring at Jason. "You might learn a thing or two. And my sister's name is *B*. Not 'Hornet.'" Dawn glanced at the book, then handed it back to B. Her high school friends laughed at Jason's stunned expression.

B wished she could disguise herself as an empty bus seat and vanish. It was bad enough that Dawn saw her rhyming dictionary and that Jason would spend all day plotting ways to get even. But the worst part was that everyone on the bus was staring at her. She hated it when people stared. Still, Dawn had stuck up for her. That was better than a poke in the eye with a sharp mascara wand.

In first period art class, B secretly tried to trans-form a clay piggy bank into a toad, but it kept collapsing. In second period history, the teacher, Miss Taykin, assigned a three-page essay on the Salem witch trials. Like everyone else at school, Miss Taykin had no idea that for B, the subject was personal.

B was so depressed by the time the bell rang for third period that she almost forgot where she was going. Then she remembered. English! Her favorite class. Her first class of the day with George.

George had lived next door to B since preschool, and they did everything together. Well, *almost* everything. Anything witch-related, B had to keep a secret. But it wasn't like she was keeping a secret from George, since she didn't appear to have witching powers anyway.

She plopped down in her seat beside George. He was a head taller than any other sixth-grader, with his crazy curly blond hair spilling over his glasses, and, as always, a Wilmington Warlocks soccer jersey worn over his T-shirt.

"Hey, B," George said. He looked around for their teacher, Mr. Bell, then slipped B his open package of Enchanted Chocolate Nuggets.

"Ahhh," B said, "just what I needed. Thanks." She took a huge handful.

"Got a new joke for you," George said. "How do you fix a flat pumpkin?"

"Um . . . how?" It was hard to talk with a mouthful of chocolate.

"With a pumpkin patch!"

B swallowed. "That's pretty good."

George mimed shooting a basket. "Two points for me," George said. "Got another one: What happens when a ghost gets lost in the fog?"

B shook her head. "I give up."

"He is mist!"

B grinned. George always cheered her up. "Where'd you get these?"

George popped some Nuggets in his mouth. "Found a Halloween joke book in the attic."

Just then Jason Jameson came into the room and B remembered the bus incident.

"Uh-oh," George said. "That's not your happy face. What's the matter?"

There wasn't much about her horrible day she could tell George. Except for one thing.

"It's Jason," she began. "He was being mean on the bus this morning."

"And I heard he shut a fourth-grader in his

locker before second period." George shook his head.

B fumed. Why did Jason have to be so horrible?

Just then, her ears caught the sound of Mozart, the class hamster, squeaking in his cage. She turned to see that Jason had the top off and was prodding Mozart with a pencil.

"Jason Jameson." B jumped out of her seat, storming over. "Leave poor Mozart *alone!*"

B grabbed for the lid to the cage, ready to force it back on.

"Hey, these guys are going to fight," shouted Jenny Springbranch, who sat next to the cage. The other kids all stood up to see.

Just then, the lights in the room flickered off and on. A man stood by the door, his hand on the switch.

Jason hid his pencil behind his back.

B stared at the man. He was taller and leaner than Mr. Bell, with a black goatee that curled to a point, and quick, darting eyes that seemed to take everything in. His clothes were dark, just like his narrow horn-rimmed glasses and cowboy boots. Something about him reminded B of Nightshade, her cat.

"What's going on here?" he asked, his eyes resting on B.

B suddenly realized she was standing there holding the lid to Mozart's cage like she was ready to whack Jason in the face with it. This did *not* look good.

"Everyone, sit." The man didn't yell, but his voice was stern. The kids filed back to their seats.

"Are you a sub?" Jenny Springbranch asked.

The man shook his head, still watching Jason and B. Jason pointed an accusing finger at B, as if she were the one who had started the trouble, and slipped back into his seat. B replaced the lid to Mozart's cage and returned to her desk, still angry, but also hoping she wasn't going to get into trouble.

"Nice job, Bumble," Jason muttered as B passed his desk.

The man walked over to the chalkboard and started writing in the upper left corner.

"Mr. Bishop," he wrote, and turned back and faced the class. "I'm Mr. Bell's replacement."

A few kids whistled in surprise. B felt a stab of worry for her old teacher, Mr. Bell. He had been her favorite. He recommended that she borrow *Through the Looking Glass* from the library.

"Now, don't worry," Mr. Bishop said. "Mr. Bell is just fine. But he won't be coming back. He's in Hawaii on an extended vacation. After twenty years of trying, his lucky lottery numbers finally hit the jackpot."

A bunch of kids started cheering. Was that because they were happy Mr. Bell got rich, or happy that he wouldn't be coming back? B couldn't tell. She knew one thing — now she was stuck with a teacher who already thought she was trouble.

Chapter 3

Mr. Bishop rubbed his hands together. "All right, class, it's time we got started." He took an empty desk from the back of the room and carried it high over his head to the front of the room, where he set it down on the floor.

"Behold! An empty desk," he said. "How many books are on this desk?"

A few kids chuckled. "None," someone called from the back.

Mr. Bishop looked surprised. "Are you sure? I could have sworn I put some books here. . . ." He pantomimed searching for books on the desk.

A few more kids laughed, as if their new teacher had a screw loose.

"You there, young man," he said, pointing to George. "Will you come up here and examine this desk and make sure it has no books *at all*?"

George grinned. "Sure." He went to the desk, waved his arm all around. "No books. No nothing," he said.

Mr. Bishop shook his head. "Just as I feared. Thank you." George sat back down, tucking his knees under his own desk with effort, he was so tall.

"This leaves me no choice, I'm afraid." Mr. Bishop pulled a large polka-dot handkerchief from his pocket. He held it up like a bullfighter's cape in front of the desk. "Abracadabra, abrakazam!" he cried and, flicking the scarf away, revealed a stack of a dozen books.

For a moment everyone was stunned silent, then the class erupted with spontaneous applause, even B.

"How'd you do that?" Kim Silsby asked. "Are you a magician?"

"Oh, I learned a few tricks in college," Mr. Bishop said, bowing modestly. "It's nothing. I could teach them to you sometime." He gestured toward the stack of books. "Books have their own type of magic. A great way to get to know someone is to find out what they're reading. Who wants to tell us about the book they're reading?"

B was so charmed by Mr. Bishop that she nearly raised her hand. Instead, she shoved it under her leg and sat on it.

Jason waved his hand in the air. "*I* have one, Mr. Bishop," he said.

Mr. Bishop checked his class list. "And your name is . . . Jameson. Jason Rudolph Jameson. Well, Mr. Jameson, tell me something you've read lately."

George and B exchanged grinning glances. *Rudolph?*

"*Stuart Little*," Jason said, looking smug.

Mr. Bishop nodded, strolling down the aisle toward where Jason sat. "An excellent choice. I should think, then, if you enjoyed a book with a mouse hero, you would learn to empathize with small rodents, and not antagonize them." He rested one hand on Mozart's cage.

Jason suddenly became very interested in a speck of paper on his desk.

B bit her lip to squash a laugh.

"How about poetry? Does anyone here like poetry?" Mr. Bishop wandered back up to the chalkboard. After what happened to Jason, no one dared to speak. Except, of course, Mr. Bishop.

"Here's a piece of a poem I like. The greatest bit of nonsense in the English language:

Beware the Jabberwock, my son!
The jaws that bite, the claws that catch!
Beware the Jubjub bird, and shun
The . . ."

He paused, and rubbed his chin. "How does it end again?"

B popped up tall in her seat. *"Frumious Bandersnatch!"* she cried. She loved that poem. It was in *Through the Looking Glass*. Then, realizing what she'd done, she scooched even lower in her seat than before. George gave her a reassuring thumbs-up.

Mr. Bishop tapped a finger on her desk. "That's

right, Beatrix," he said, again referring to his class list. "Nicely done." B felt a bit lighter. Maybe her day was getting better.

"Which reminds me . . ." He hurried to Mr. Bell's desk and returned with a stack of papers. "Mr. Bell left these for you. They're your grades on last week's oral book reports. Sarah? Sarah Aarons? There you are. Jamal Burns? Here you are, Mr. Burns. Lisa Donahue?" And around the room he went.

Jason got his paper back, and held it up high like a boxing championship belt to show everyone his A. Nobody cared. George got an A, too, but he just put his paper away in his English folder. Last of all, Mr. Bishop placed B's report on her desk. He bent down and said, in a low voice, "You're going to have to do better than this."

B glanced at her paper.

She got a *D*.

A D, in English, her best subject!

And all because she got so nervous when everyone stared at her, just like on the bus this morning. She hated speaking or even reading in front of other people.

Her D blinked at her like a flashing traffic light. Great. Now her amazing new English teacher thought she was both a troublemaker *and* a poor student. She turned the paper facedown and closed her eyes tight to block out her embarrassment.

"B for Beatrix, D for dummy," Jason Jameson whispered. She turned to glare at him, but by then he was facing the teacher again, looking like he had a halo hovering over his head.

Mr. Bishop went back to the blackboard. "If we're here to learn English, let's start with the basics," he said. He picked up the chalk and wrote "W-O-R-D-S" on the board. "Words," he said. "The building blocks of the English language. And that means spelling! Who wants to have a class spelling contest?"

Some kids groaned, but B's spirits lifted. Spelling was one thing she knew she could do well. Words just stuck in her brain, once she'd read them a few times. She naturally invented little tricks to memorize difficult spellings. B wanted Mr. Bishop to know that she loved words as much as he did. And here was her chance.

"Best of all," Mr. Bishop said, pulling two small pieces of paper out of his wallet, "the winner takes a prize: two front-row tickets with backstage passes to the upcoming Black Cats concert!"

Holy cats! B thought. Black Cats tickets?

Kids squealed and cheered. Jason pumped his fist in the air. Even George sat up taller. But B was already forming a study plan. Those tickets were as good as hers.

Mr. Bishop went to his desktop computer and printed something, then came back to the front of the room. "This is the list," he said, waving the paper in the air. "Two hundred and fifty juicy words. That should keep us busy. Wouldn't you like to know what they are?" He grinned, then tucked the list away in a black folder. "We'll practice them tomorrow."

Jenny Springbranch shot her hand in the air. "Excuse me, Mr. Bishop," she said.

"Yes, Jenny?"

"Did you just say this spelling test will have *two hundred and fifty* words?"

Mr. Bishop looked surprised. "It's not a test. It's

going to be a spelling *bee*. Everyone will take their turn, standing here in front of the class, spelling their word out loud."

B deflated like a week-old helium balloon. Out loud? In front of the whole class?

"You'll only need to know the words you're given," Mr. Bishop said. "Problem is, there's no way to tell what they'll be."

He found a thumbtack and stuck the two tickets to the bulletin board on the side wall.

"Keep an eye on these for me, will you, Mozart?" he joked.

B felt her stomach flutter. Oh, she wanted those tickets! But how could she stand in front of the class and spell well enough to win?

She stared at the white tickets printed with "Black Cats" in big, bold type. She'd never wanted any prize so badly.

She could read the dictionary. She could review her entire spelling notebook. She could stay up late every night studying. But standing up in front of others — well, there was nothing that could prepare her for that horror.

B clenched her fists. If only she had her magic and could work a spell to eliminate stage fright.

But she couldn't.

She'd have to earn those tickets the hard way.

As usual.

Chapter 4

When B got home, all she wanted was peace and quiet. She'd had enough attention for one day. She wanted to disappear to her room and study her spelling words. But as usual, she heard laughter coming from upstairs. Dawn was always on the phone.

Maybe her first spell would be to conjure magic earplugs. B tiptoed upstairs, as quiet as Nightshade tracking a mouse. She knew better than to disturb her sister.

When she reached the hallway landing, she paused. Several girl voices came from Dawn's room, not to mention colorful splashes of light spilling out under the door, and tinkling sounds, and per-fumey smells.

Dawn was practicing magic — she just knew it. B pressed her face against the keyhole and peeked in. Maybe she could learn a tip or two from her big sister. But all she could see was the back of someone's head — someone with sleek black hair. Definitely not Dawn, or any of Dawn's friends that B had met before.

"Ooh! Mahvelous, dahling!" Dawn's voice said. "You look like a star!" And several voices laughed.

If only I had magic, B thought, *I could think up a rhyme to spy on Dawn unnoticed.* She got an idea, and whispered:

"I'm wishin', I'm prayin', I'm dreamin', I'm hopin'
My magic will start and that door will fly open."

Nothing happened. B wasn't surprised, but she smiled — at least a little. Even if it wasn't magical, the rhyme was pretty clever. And that was magic, of a sort.

But it still didn't give her a view of what was going on in there.

"Me next," a voice from inside Dawn's room said. "I've got a good one."

A good one *what*? Curiosity was killing B. *It figures*, she thought. She'd probably never find out. Just like everything else today — all she had to show for her efforts was frustration.

She scooched her eye closer to the keyhole. *"C'mon, open,"* she whispered. Her mind flashed to Mr. Bishop's classroom and tomorrow's spelling bee practice. "O-P-E-N."

She leaned her head against the doorknob.

It turned, just a little, and the latch clicked.

B was thrown off balance. She tumbled forward into the room. She caught a glimpse of four startled teen girls' faces staring up at her, right before she tripped over Nightshade and toppled to the floor.

Nightshade yowled.

The girls laughed.

B picked herself up and brushed carpet fuzz from her face. She dreaded looking back at Dawn, but there was no avoiding it. Dawn's blue eyes flashed with annoyance, but she kept her face from showing it. To her friends, she was a calm, mature big sister. Especially to *these* friends, who must be new. Dawn always found a way to look good. That was another one of the family talents that B hadn't inherited.

"Is this your little sister, Dawn?" the girl with the shiny black hair said. She was dressed all in black and looked really sophisticated, maybe older than Dawn.

B saw three sets of strangers' eyes watching her like she was a hamster in a cage. Her tongue went dry.

Dawn nodded. "This is B. Short for Beatrix. She's in sixth grade."

"Hey, B," the girl said. "I'm Angela." A sparkly silver bracelet on Angela's wrist stood out against the dark clothes. The bracelet B still hadn't received. Witches only got their charm bracelets when they got their magic and started their lessons. Angela had two charms, one shaped like a diamond and the other like a tiny cauldron.

Another girl with short, spiky brown hair nodded knowingly. Her brightly colored T-shirt matched the rainbow colors in her wild eye makeup. But she, too, wore a bracelet with two charms.

"Yo, B," the girl said. "I'm Stef. Sixth grade, eh? What does that make you, ten?"

"Eleven," B said quickly. Then she realized her mistake as Stef's gaze went toward her bare wrists. At eleven, she ought to have her magic.

"No bracelet, huh?" Stef observed.

B felt her face get hot.

"Hers is broken," Dawn said. "Dad's got it so he can fix the clasp."

B turned sharply and stared at Dawn. Her sister's cheeks were pink, but her face was defiant.

"Geez, Stef," a tall girl with glasses and dark red hair said. "You're embarrassing her."

"There's nothing embarrassing," Dawn said, looking directly at B. "B has her magic."

B got the picture — Dawn didn't want her friends to know that her sister was a magical freak.

"Excellent!" the red-haired girl said, fingering her own bracelet, which had a flower, a cat, and a cloud charm. B wondered what the significance of each charm was. "I'm Macey. You sit down, and let's see if your newbie magic can get these complicated spells to last longer than a minute." The girl grinned at Stef. "After all, Stef can't manage it. . . ."

"Hey!" Stef said. She whapped Macey with a fuzzy pink pillow. Both of them giggled. Macey threw the pillow back at Stef.

B knew that beginner's magic didn't always last, but hers didn't even start.

"Uh, well," Dawn said. "It might not work —"

Macey interrupted, "When my brother first got his magic, his fourth spell lasted a whole week!"

"Let's just try it," Angela suggested, smiling at B and patting a spot on the floor where she could sit. For the first time, B noticed a big pink handbag sitting open in the middle of the circle where the girls all sat cross-legged, and a pile of random objects next to each girl. "We're doing magical makeovers. Want us to make you glamorous?"

"Um," B finally managed to speak. "No, thanks." She caught sight of Dawn's frown. "I'd better go. I've got homework. . . ."

"Overruled," Angela said. "Your presence is requested by a unanimous vote. Right, girls?"

"Right," Macey said.

"Sure," Stef said.

Everyone turned to look at Dawn. She blinked, then shrugged. "She can stay if she wants," she said.

And before B could think up a way to escape, they'd pulled her onto a cushion on the floor beside them.

Macey laughed and gave B a sideways hug. "Watch and learn, my little witchy friend," she said. "Then it'll be your turn."

This spells disaster, B thought. She gritted her teeth and prayed that she'd make it through the next few minutes without embarrassing her sister and herself.

Chapter 5

"Watch closely, B," Angela said, pointing to the pink bag on the floor. "I'm going to show you some beauty tips."

Stef leaned over and flicked on Dawn's stereo. The latest Black Cats song, "Yowl," filled the room. Angela rummaged through her pile of stuff on the floor and selected a handful of small objects. B craned her neck to see what they were.

"Okay." Angela gestured to Stef. "Do you think I can turn this punk goddess into a fashion supermodel?"

"Uh . . ." B didn't dare answer.

"Pay attention, B," Angela said. "You might learn something. First of all, did you know that even a purse can be a cauldron? And not every concoction is liquid. All those messy, stinky brews, ugh!" Tossing a blue Christmas bauble into her bag, she said:

"Like Rapunzel's — grow, hair, grow!
Long and thick, highlights aglow."

Stef's short brown spikes elongated. B's jaw dropped. She'd seen magic before, of course, but Mom and Dad never did stuff like this!

Stef shook her head, and a thick head of wavy, shiny hair spilled over her shoulders. This was way stronger stuff than Dawn's eyelash enhancer.

"Wow!" B said. *Grow, aglow.* She never would have thought of that rhyme.

"I'm just getting started," Angela said. She tossed a smooth, beach-polished stone into the pink bag.

"Cleanser, toner, beauty cream,
My magic facial makes skin gleam."

The wild-colored makeup vanished from Stef's face. Her pimples and freckles disappeared, and her cheeks took on a smooth, healthy shine. Macey and Dawn applauded.

Stef examined herself in a mirror. "That's not me, is it?" she said. "I feel naked without my purple eyeliner."

Angela rolled her eyes. She sprinkled a pinch of glitter, a handful of buttons, and two red feathers into the pink bag.

"Magic beauty is such a breeze
With the right makeup and accessories."

Stef closed her eyes while invisible brushes and wands stroked cosmetics over her face. Her pirate skull and crossbones earrings shrank and turned into diamonds, with a necklace and bracelet to match.

"Holy cats!" B said. "Those rhymes made you gorgeous!"

"Don't sound so surprised," Stef said, sticking out her tongue.

"But you've got to admit, the jewelry doesn't exactly fit the clothes," Macey said, pointing to Stef's camouflage shorts and high-top sneakers.

"Leave that to me," Angela said. "Stand up, Stef." She reached over toward Dawn's desk and grabbed a tissue, which she dropped into the bag, followed by the most recent issue of *Vogue*, a can of Coke, and a bottle of children's bubbles.

"Italian shoes, designer gown, with style in every
stitch.
The secret's out: A fairy godmom's just a stylish
witch!"

And in a twinkle of pink light, Stef's punk clothes disappeared, and in their place was a long, elegant silver evening gown. Stef, standing taller in her strappy high heels, gasped when she saw herself in Dawn's door mirror.

B shook her head in amazement. *That* was some gifted rhyming.

"Bravo, Angela!" Dawn cried.

Stef held out a hand to get everyone's attention. She tossed a paper clip into the bag and said:

"Dress and makeup, fine. So are jewels from
Tiffany's.
Now tweak this look so it's still hot, yet also
Stephanie's."

Her diamond necklace turned into a black pearl choker. The hem of the silver evening gown rose to knee-height and turned frayed and jagged. Her strappy silver heels transformed into tall black leather boots.

Macey let out a wolf whistle, then giggled. Angela frowned slightly. She clearly preferred Stef's original look.

"There it goes," Macey said, pointing to Stef's hair. It was *un*-growing, retracting back into her head. Her movie-star makeup changed back to purple and green, and she grew shorter as her leather boots transformed into canvas high-top sneakers. With a puff of smoke, the old Stef stood before them. She took a bow, and laughed.

"If only the spell could last," Stef said.

"No kidding," Macey said. But everyone knew that only adult witches who'd passed all their classes could make complicated spells last — or newbies with accidental power surges.

"Angela," Dawn said. "That was incredible. You need to do that in the spelling competition!"

B blinked. Spelling competition? "You mean high school kids have spelling bees, too?"

The girls wore puzzled expressions. Then Stef giggled.

"No, silly," she said. "We don't mean spelling like A-B-C spelling. We mean magical spelling. You know, making up spells?"

B wanted to disappear. If she had her powers, she would have known all about spelling competitions.

"They hold the competition every year at the Magical Rhyming Society," Dawn explained, as if it was perfectly normal not to know.

"Hey, B, let's see what you can do," Stef said. "Make up a bag-cauldron concoction to turn me into a supermodel again."

B panicked. She opened her mouth to say she couldn't, then clamped it shut again. There had to be a way out of this mess! But before she could think up an answer, Dawn spoke.

"*Nobody* could top Angela," she said. "B's only eleven, for heaven's sake. Her magic is too new for that. Let's play Truth or Dare, okay? Anyway, B probably needs to go start her homework. Don't you, B?"

B nodded, for once in her life grateful that her big sister was kicking her out of her bedroom.

"Phooey," Stef said. "How much homework can a kid her age have? I've got tons, and that doesn't stop me."

"Yeah, Dawn, let your sister stay," Macey said. "I want to see what the cute little newbie can do."

B knew that Macey meant to be nice, but right then she wished *she* had a pillow to throw at her.

"B goes first," Angela said. "Truth or dare, B?"

B tried to think, but it was so hard with all those eyes watching her. If she chose truth, and they asked her questions about her magic, then she'd really be in trouble. If she chose dare, they might ask her to do something embarrassing, bark like a seal or something, but that would be better than *really* embarrassing herself.

"Dare," she said, her hands sweating.

"Dare it is," Angela said.

"I've got one," Stef said. "I dare you, B, to turn yourself into an animal."

B glanced helplessly at Dawn.

"Don't be shy, B," Dawn said.

What? B tried to read what Dawn's eyes were telling her, but all her sister did was nod encouragingly. "Just think of your favorite animal, put a few objects into the bag, and say a rhyme," she said.

"Nothing man-eating, okay?" Macey added.

"Ha-ha," B said, unconvincingly. Her throat was dry. It was hard enough to think of an animal, much less a rhyme. If only this were a class assignment, not a public performance . . .

B's mind drifted back to English class, and the couplet Mr. Bishop had read. No, she decided, she'd better not rhyme about the Jabberwock, just in case it did work this time. She'd better settle for Mozart the hamster. He was harmless enough.

Hamster. Dumpster? Not quite. Amster-dam? Hamster, clamster, "Fry with Pam"-ster.

She had no idea what to choose, but she picked up a little white bead from Angela's pile and a piece of ribbon from Stef's pile and put them in the bag. Then she said:

"Tiny nose, and ears, and paws . . ."

B licked her lips, then realized Dawn's lips were moving, too. She was repeating B's words softly.

"Soft fur that hides my scratchy claws!"

That could be anything, B realized. A mouse, a gerbil, a guinea pig. But it was too late to change it. B could feel her nose shrinking! And her ears, and her hands and feet, and all of her, sinking down toward the ground, her head coming low to the carpet as her body turned from two-legged to four-legged. It hurt! Well, not hurt, exactly, but B didn't like it. Her skin sprouted soft, gray fur that made her want to sneeze. And strangest of all was the sensation near her lower back — it was a long tail, twitching. She was a mouse!

"Make it stop!" she tried to say to Dawn, but all that came out was "peep-pe-peep." And Dawn! She was gigantic! Monster Dawn, with her monster sidekicks, all of whom were making cooing noises and reaching out their tree-size hands to try to pet . . . her!

B scurried under a chair, panting. What if the spell couldn't be undone and she was stuck in a mouse's body forever? Her heart beat wildly.

"Better come on out of there," Stef's voice boomed in B's mouse ears.

Before mouse B could respond, the room seemed to shrink, and something bonked her in the head. It was the rungs of the chair, which toppled from B crouching underneath it.

B blinked at the sight of Dawn's friends, normal-size once more. She blinked again. They were applauding her!

"That was amazing, B," Macey said, beaming. "I was thirteen at least before I could do a cauldron-bag spell."

"Yeah," Stef said. "I tried to turn my brother into a frog when I was your age, but all I got was a single ribbit. You must be gifted or something."

"You'll get your first charm in no time," Angela said. They all smiled, and B smiled back, but her heart wasn't in it.

It hurt to take their compliments, knowing that really, she had as much magic in her as a licorice whip.

She stood up and put on a brave face. "Thanks for letting me hang out," she told Dawn's friends.

"I've got to get started on my spelling homework. Nice to meet you all."

B went into her room, feeling awful. Would she have to go through life *pretending* she had magic? What was wrong with her?

Chapter 6

The next day when B walked into English class, the first thing she saw were the tickets to the Black Cats concert pinned to the bulletin board. And she wasn't the only one. A cluster of students jostled near the board.

"These tickets are worth a fortune!" Jason Jameson said.

"Mr. Bishop must know somebody connected to the band," Kim Silsby said.

"Well, I'm going to win them," Jason declared. "I practiced spelling for two hours last night."

B had done a lot more than that. She'd stayed up late copying words by hand. But she knew she couldn't prepare for all that . . . staring. She sank into her chair. Adding to her worries was the fact that she was still magic-less. That morning, she'd tried to fill Nightshade's bowl with a brilliant twist on "cat food" and "bad mood," but no luck.

"Hey, B," George said, sitting next to her and holding out a bag of Enchanted Chocolate Mint Fizzes. "Got one for you. What do witches put on their hair?"

"Huh?" B said, startled.

"Scare spray!" he cried, laughing. "Get it? *Scare spray?*"

B breathed a sigh of relief, and reached for a chocolate. "I get it," she said. "From your Halloween joke book, right?"

George nodded.

"I like the ghost one better," B said.

George shrugged and popped a Mint Fizz in his mouth. "You ready for the practice round?"

"Hope so," she said, watching her classmates drool over the tickets.

Tickets, she thought. *Think of the tickets. You can do this. Maybe you can't cast spells, but you can spell.*

"I wanna hold them," Jason was saying, reaching for the thumbtack that held the tickets in place.

"Mr. Jameson." Mr. Bishop's warning voice came from the doorway. "Hands off, please. Nobody touches those tickets until I hand them to the class spelling champion. Understood?"

Mr. Bishop was dressed in dark red today — red pants, even! But he still wore those black cowboy boots.

"Yes, sir," Jason said meekly, returning to his seat like a perfect student.

"Take your seats, let's get settled," Mr. Bishop said. "Anybody absent? All seats filled? Good!" He rubbed his hands together. "See this, class?" Mr. Bishop held up one finger. "This is my magic pointer. It will tell us who should go first." Tying his polka-dot handkerchief around his eyes, he staggered around the room, pointing wildly.

Everyone laughed, including B, until Mr. Bishop stopped, with his magic finger pointed right at her. "Beatrix!" he cried, peeking out from under his scarf. "You're numero uno!"

"Um, Mr. Bishop?" It was George's voice.

"Yes?"

"She's B," George said. "She doesn't like to be called Beatrix, really. Everyone calls her B."

"I stand corrected," he said. "What do you say, B, want to kick off our spelling bee? You've got the name for it."

Well, she might as well get this over with. "Okay," she said.

She stood and shuffled to the front of the room. She tried not to look at the sea of faces staring at her. She focused on her slightly grubby sneakers instead.

"Here's how it works. I say the word. You repeat it, you spell it, then repeat it again. So, if I were given the word 'cat,' I'd do this: 'Cat. C-A-T. Cat.' Got it?"

B nodded.

"The first word is . . ." Mr. Bishop paused dramatically, "'scratchy.'"

That's easy, B thought. She'd been gearing up for something like "dentifrice," which was a fancy way of saying toothpaste.

"B? Are you with us?" Mr. Bishop asked.

"Sorry," B stammered, catching sight of the class staring at her. She was determined to ignore the panic rising up in her stomach. Her hands were beginning to sweat. "Scratchy. S-C-R-A . . ."

Jason coughed loudly. He stared straight at her, mouthing "Loser," but of course Mr. Bishop couldn't see. Darn him! She looked away. George's blond head stood tall above the others, nodding encouragingly at her. Jenny Springbranch smirked like she expected she'd win herself. B felt her heart thumping and had to stop herself from running back to her seat.

Where had she been? "C-H-Y. Scratchy," she said in a rush, and hurried toward her seat.

"I'm sorry, B, but that's incorrect," Mr. Bishop said.

What?

"Since this is practice only," her teacher went on, "does anyone here think they can spell that word correctly?"

"I can, Mr. Bishop!" Jason Jameson was hovering over his chair, waving his hand high in the air.

"All right, Mr. Jameson, come up here and show us what you can do."

Jason reached the chalkboard and turned around. He bent at the knees like a baboon and scratched his hair with one hand, his ribs with another, all the while leering at B. "Scratchy," he said. "S-C-R-A-*T*-C-H-Y. Scratchy."

"That's right," Mr. Bishop said. "And thank you for the demonstration as well."

Jason scratched a few more times on his way back to his seat and whispered, "Loser," as he passed.

B caught George's eye, and whispered, "Isn't that what I said?"

George shook his head sadly. "You dropped the 'T.'"

B slumped down low in her seat. Such an easy word, and she flubbed it. She felt queasy. Jason was totally cheating by distracting her, but if she wasn't so scared of standing up in class, he wouldn't be able to get to her. It was so frustrating!

They went around the room, taking turns spelling words. B spelled every word correctly in her head, even the ones that others tripped on, like "believe" and "recommend" and "exaggerate." She knew all the rules about "i before e," and nearly all the exceptions, too. By the time her turn came around again, B was so angry at her mistake, and at Jason's teasing her, she was ready, even if it meant braving the staring faces.

"Disguise," Mr. Bishop said, watching her closely.

She closed her eyes and thought about the Black Cats tickets. Then she pictured the word "disguise," just as it would appear on a printed page.

"Disguise. D-I-S-G-U-I-S-E," she said, a smile tugging at her lips. B knew she had nailed it. "Disguise."

"That's right," Mr. Bishop said. But B already knew that. She made sure to give Jason a triumphant look before sitting down.

The rest of the kids took their second turns, but B didn't bother spelling their words in her head anymore. She'd proven her point. She could spell with the best of them.

"One more round, then we'll wrap it up," Mr.

Bishop said. "I'll turn on some Black Cats tunes while you complete this week's section in your vocab workbook. Deal?" Everyone cheered. "B, you're up."

B walked to the front of the room. It was getting a little easier every time.

"Chaos," Mr. Bishop said.

At least it's short, B thought. Jason did more of his ridiculous scratching at her from his seat, but she was determined not to let him get to her. She looked up and focused on the ceiling tiles.

"Chaos," she said, picturing the word in bold, black letters in her mind's eye. "C-H-A-O-S. Chaos."

"That's right," Mr. Bishop said.

Just then, two big drips of moisture landed on B's head. She touched her hair and looked up in time to see the overhead sprinklers kick into high gear and blast the classroom with water.

Sploosh!

Everyone gasped and squealed and held their arms over their heads. The showering water sounded like an indoor rainstorm.

Meeep — meeep — meeep . . . The fire alarm began blaring, its warning strobe lights flashing in the classroom ceiling and down the corridors. Warning bells chimed from the loudspeaker, and the principal's voice came on.

"Teachers will lead their classes out to their designated safe spots," he said. "This is not a scheduled fire drill. I repeat, this is not a scheduled fire drill."

Chapter 7

"Do you think there's a real fire?" B asked George as they filed through the corridors, the alarm ringing deafeningly overhead.

George sniffed the air. "I don't smell any smoke." He elbowed B. "Here's one you'll like: What did the fireman say when the church caught on fire?"

Leave it to George to make jokes at a time like this! "What?"

"Holy smoke!" George laughed to himself again.

Classes streamed out of every room, hurrying outdoors. Usually during a fire drill the students would joke about the noise and the inconvenience. But now the teachers moved quickly and looked serious, not to mention wet. The sprinklers had gone off throughout the entire building. Mrs. Fox, the librarian, looked ready to murder someone.

They exited onto the soccer fields under the bright noonday sun. B had to shield her eyes. Mr. Bishop passed behind her, striding up and down the length of his class's line of students, counting heads and muttering to himself.

"Someone's missing," Mr. Bishop said loudly. "Class, please stand still while I count again."

Just then the fire truck swung into view and disappeared behind the school.

"It's Jason," Kim called out from the end of the row. "He's not here."

Mr. Bishop turned toward the school, but before he took off running, out staggered Jason, clutching Mozart's hamster cage.

Jenny started clapping. "Jason's a hero!" she cried. "He saved Mozart!"

She seemed to expect the rest of the class to join in her applause, but no one did. Mr. Bishop relieved Jason of the cage, then said, loud enough for the whole class to hear, "It was extremely irresponsible of you to linger in the classroom during the fire alarm. Especially when you heard the principal's warning."

Jason stuck out his lower lip. "I . . . I was afraid of something bad happening to Mozart."

B and George exchanged a glance. Just yesterday he was torturing the poor hamster. B wasn't convinced by Jason's heroics, and neither, she could tell, was George. He must have been up to something.

Finally, the principal announced that there was no fire and it was safe to return. One by one, the classes straggled back in. George went on ahead, chatting with Jamal about last night's soccer game, but B hung back to hold the door open for Mr. Bishop, whose hands were tied up with Mozart's cage.

"Thanks, Beatrix. I mean, B. Sorry." He gave her a friendly nudge. "To be or not to be."

"That is the question." B knew that line of dialogue because her mom said it to her all the time.

"Do you know where the quote is from?" Mr. Bishop glanced at B out of the corner of his eye.

"William Shakespeare wrote it," B said, stepping up her pace to keep up with Mr. Bishop. "It's from *Hamlet.*"

Mr. Bishop smiled. "Any student who can quote from plays and poetry is all right in my book."

B felt a flutter of pride. She stood a little taller. "I do like to rhyme."

"Magnificent!" Mr. Bishop said. "When this spelling business is finished, I plan on a poetry unit. Tell me, do you make up any rhymes of your own?"

B had to swallow a laugh. If only he knew! "I try," she said. "But they don't really work."

They reached Mr. Bishop's classroom. B's class was gathering up their bags and books, which were damp from the fire alarm sprinklers.

Things were looking up. Maybe Mr. Bishop didn't think she was a total loser. And she decided that she wanted to win the spelling competition even more to impress him. With a little luck, the

Black Cats tickets would be hers. B glanced at the bulletin board, where the tickets were pinned.

Except, they weren't.

B gasped.

Jenny Springbranch had noticed, too. "Oh! Oh! Mr. Bishop!" she cried, pointing to the bare thumbtack. "Someone stole the spelling bee prize!"

Chapter 8

Mr. Bishop stopped in the doorway, his eyes scanning the room, his brow furrowed. B thought she saw his lips move, as if he was muttering to himself. The tip of his beard waggled.

"Does anybody have anything they'd like to tell me?" he said, looking from student to student.

B had never heard a class this quiet.

"It wasn't easy getting those tickets," Mr. Bishop said, pacing up and down the aisles. "I thought it would be worth the effort, though, to have something exciting to motivate you to do your very best on this spelling bee. But this . . ." He pointed to the ticketless bulletin board. "I'm very disappointed."

B felt her insides squirm as though she were guilty. And she hadn't done anything wrong! Teachers' lectures always made her feel jittery.

The bell to end the period rang.

"I have to dismiss you now," Mr. Bishop said, "but I'm going to investigate the disappearance of those tickets fully, mark my words. It would be far better for the person who took them to return them to me and apologize. Do you all understand?"

Twenty heads nodded. Twenty pairs of eyes stared at their shoes.

Mr. Bishop opened the door. "See you tomorrow."

B hung back toward the end of the line of kids filing out the door, her mind a whirl. Black Cats tickets, stolen. Who'd have the nerve to do such a thing?

George fell into step beside her, his eyes wide with astonishment. The rest of her classmates had scattered off to lockers and lunch, leaving the hallway nearly empty.

"I've got to stop at my locker and pick up some more chocolate," George said. "I'll meet you in the caf."

"How can you possibly think of chocolate at a time like this?" B said. "We've got to find out who took those tickets."

"Well, I can't think on an empty stomach," George said. "See you in a minute."

George headed off toward his locker, and B wandered toward the cafeteria. As she rounded a corner she stopped short. Jason Jameson! Standing alone, in the middle of the hall, looking both ways. B ducked out of sight and peeked back around the corner.

He opened his backpack, looked inside it, and giggled to himself.

Holy cats! Now *there* was suspicious behavior.

Who would be more likely to steal tickets than Jason Jameson? Jason often took cookies off other kids' lunch trays in the cafeteria.

But how could he have managed to steal the tickets?

The fire drill! Of course! When everyone else left the room, he stayed back, supposedly to rescue Mozart. The hamster that he always picked on.

He's the only one who's been alone with the tickets.

And now, there he stood, staring in his backpack and chuckling to himself like he'd gotten away with something.

B had to act, before he really did.

"Hey, Jason," B called, stepping into view. Jason jumped, then quickly zipped his backpack shut.

"Whatcha hiding in that bag?" B called, catching up to where he stood.

"Oh, nothing, Bumble B," he said, sneering. "Just something . . . *scratchy.*"

B took a deep breath. "I *can* spell scratchy, and I *would* have if you hadn't messed me up. S-C-R-A-T-C-H-Y. See?"

"Ooh, you're sooo smart," Jason said. He scratched his chest hard. Then he dropped his backpack and scratched all over his body like an orangutan.

B groaned. "I am so sick of your teasing," she

said. "Scratch yourself silly. I'm not sticking around to watch." And she stomped off down the hall and hurried to the cafeteria.

George caught up with her, sprinting like it was track and field day.

"You know what I think?" B told him as he skidded to a stop beside her.

"What?"

B dropped her voice to a whisper. "I think Jason Jameson took the Black Cats tickets." And B told George all she'd seen, and how Jason had reacted.

George whistled. "That skunk! It's just like something he'd do. But how can we prove it?"

B pressed her lips together. If only she had her magic, this could be so easy.

Still, magic or no magic, she would make those tickets reappear.

"I'll find a way," she said. "You watch."

Chapter 9

They arrived at the cafeteria and picked up trays and utensils at the end of the line. Most of the other kids had already gotten their food, so they didn't have to wait.

"Let's see . . ." George said, scanning the menu. "Dog food meat loaf with peas."

"Compared to my mom's meat loaf, it might as well be dog food," B said.

"Your mom is the best cook in the universe," George said reverently.

"I'd rather be the best speller in the universe," B said. "The tickets might be gone temporarily, but I'm going to get them back, and then I'm going to win them! Quiz me."

George pointed to the steaming tray of meat loaf to tell the lunch lady what he wanted. "Spell 'carbohydrate,'" he told B.

B checked out the cardboard pizza squares. She wished the cafeteria served real food. "C-A-R-B-O-H-Y-D-R-A-T-E," B said proudly. "Beat that."

"Umm, Mrs. Gillet? I changed my mind," George said. "I'll have some of that spaghetti."

The lunch lady stared at George. She looked baffled underneath her white paper cap. "Spaghetti?"

"Right there," George said, pointing to a steaming pan full of spaghetti with huge meatballs, like a real Italian restaurant.

Mrs. Gillet shook her head and reached for a new scooper. "Marge," she called over her shoulder, "you forgot to put 'spaghetti' on the menu board this morning."

B didn't hear Marge's reply. She was trying to decide between a stale brownie or gloopy pudding on the dessert tray. "Quiz me again."

"Um . . . raspberry."

B closed her eyes to picture the word.

Rasp-berry, that was her trick. A raspy berry, prickly with tiny seeds.

"R-A-S-P-B-E-R-R-Y," she said. "Got it right, didn't I?"

George didn't answer. He stood stock-still, staring at a cookie in his hand.

"B, hon," Mrs. Gillet distracted her. "Have you decided what you want to eat?"

B pointed at George. "Sorry, Mrs. G. The same as him." She reached for a milk, then elbowed George. "What's gotten into you?"

George held out the cookie. "I could swear this had an Enchanted Chocolate Square in the middle of it a minute ago," he said. "But now it's got a jelly filling or something."

"Looks good," B said. "My mom makes something like that for parties."

They took their trays to the cash register and swiped their lunch cards. They found empty seats near the window and sat down to eat. Outside on the athletic field, the eighth-grade boys' gym class was playing soccer.

"So, you really want to win this spelling bee, huh?" George said. "All this practice spelling."

"Are you kidding? I tried to get Mom and Dad to let me go see the Black Cats last year, but by the time I'd saved up my allowance money, the tickets were long gone."

George twirled spaghetti onto his fork. "Nobody's gonna win tickets if Mr. Bishop doesn't find out who took them."

"I don't see how he could," B said. "He's new, he doesn't know people." She cut her meatball in half. "I think it's up to us. We're the ones who have it figured out."

George examined his cookie. "What is this jelly stuff? Strawberry?"

"Does it matter?" B asked. "C'mon, hit me with some more words. You haven't stumped me yet. And no more food words."

George nibbled his cookie. "Okay," he said. "Desert."

B pictured the word in her mind, just to make sure. "Dessert" had two "s"'s, for "soft" and "silky."

Like a mousse, a two-"s" dessert. "Desert," as in the Sahara, had only one "s."

She took a breath. A tall blond eighth-grader scored a long-shot goal, and the commotion outside caught her eye. The sun beating down on the grass made the green so brilliant, it dazzled her. "Desert. D-E-S-E-R-T."

George stuffed the rest of his cookie into his mouth, and slurped his milk. "Bravo."

B pretended to bow.

Just then, they heard a loud beeping horn sounding outside. They looked up to see a huge dump truck backing up right onto the midline of the soccer field. The gym teacher blew his whistle and ran toward the truck, his arms waving.

"First fire trucks, now dump trucks," B said. "What a day!"

Most of the kids in the cafeteria were clustered around the windows now.

George stood up to get a better view. "Look what they're doing, B," he said, his voice incredulous. "They're dumping *sand* right onto the soccer field!"

B stood on tiptoe. "The truck must be from that construction site over there," she said, pointing to some heavy equipment farther down the road.

"Coach is having a fit," George said. Then he snorted with laughter. "Did you realize? You just spelled 'desert,'" he said. "And now we have a desert of our own."

B halted. She stared at George.

She'd spelled "desert," and then a desert appeared?

Uh-oh.

B stared at the sand spilling from the dump truck.

Spelling?

It couldn't be! Spells were couplets. Rhymes.

Holy cats, she'd spelled tons of words since her birthday. Hadn't she?

A few minutes ago she'd spelled "carbohydrate," and . . . she gulped. *Spaghetti had appeared.* Spaghetti Mrs. Gillet was not expecting. And what about George's mysterious cookie?

"Magic," she whispered. Had it finally happened?

B had never heard of a witch whose powers worked that way. Was it even *allowed*?

She had made things happen just by spelling words.

B had her magic at last!

Chapter 10

B tried to control herself. But she couldn't help it. Her magic had finally arrived. First her toes started to tingle. Then her body wiggled. She broke out into her happy dance.

"What do you call that?" George said, mimicking her. "The Cauldron Boogie?"

B stopped midboogie. "What?"

"That little happy dance you do," George said, demonstrating, holding both fists together out in front of his chest, then swinging them round and round. "You look like a hip-hop witch stirring a cauldron."

B stammered and spluttered. "That's just silly." But she stopped dancing just in case.

Her elation faded as thoughts tumbled over each other. She had never heard of anyone casting spells without rhyming. What did it mean? Would her parents be happy that she had her magic, or did it mean she was some sort of freak?

George crumpled his empty milk carton and lobbed it into a nearby trash can. "What's made you so happy?"

Despite her worries, B couldn't wipe the grin off her face. "Oh, nothing."

"No fair," George said. "I always tell you my jokes. Want a Mint Fizz?"

"We already had cookies," she reminded him, then popped a Mint Fizz in her mouth. But she nearly choked when she saw Jason dumping his tray.

Jason paused at the cafeteria door to check if anyone was watching and slipped outside, clutching his backpack.

"C'mon! Let's not let him out of our sights," B said, grabbing her tray with one hand and George's arm with the other. "Those tickets are in his backpack. I'm sure of it."

"If he stole the Black Cats tickets," George asked, "does that make him a cat burglar?"

"Good one!" B laughed. "Come on, let's go!"

B and George ditched their trays and ran out of the cafeteria. They hurried after Jason, into the deserted hallway, trying to keep their footfalls soft and quiet on the hard tile floor. They stopped at each corner like secret agents, peering around the wall in search of Jason, then tiptoeing to the next turn.

They spotted Jason crouching in front of his locker.

"We've got to get closer," B said.

"I know!" George said. "We could disguise ourselves as bushes —"

But just then, the bell rang. Students flooded the hall, creating a barricade between them and Jason's locker.

Jason shut his backpack inside his locker and stood up.

"Darn!" B said. "We were so close!" She sighed. "C'mon, let's go to gym. We'll think of something." She made a quick mental note of which locker was his: fourth one to the left of the drinking fountain that usually blasted you in the eye.

"Look on the bright side," George said. "The tickets, if they're in his backpack, aren't going anywhere for the next period."

"Maybe I can sneak out to the bathroom during gym and get into his locker," B mused.

They barged through the double gym doors just as Mr. Lyons, the gym teacher, blew his whistle. "Listen up, troops," he said. "Today's a perfect day for playing soccer outdoors."

So much for sneaking to Jason's locker.

"However," Mr. Lyons went on, his face flushed with anger, "some gravel company apparently got us confused with a sandbox today, and they've dumped a couple tons of sand onto our playing field!"

B bit her lip. She felt a little bit guilty. *But I wasn't* trying *to ruin the soccer field. I'll have to be more careful.*

"So today, it's dodgeball, troops," Mr. Lyons said. "Split up into two teams. Don't cross the center line. Four balls in play. To the death!"

Half the class cheered. The other half groaned.

George nudged B. "Why not make your move now and dodge the dodge altogether?"

"Great idea," B said. Those big rubber balls could sting, after all.

"Can I go to the bathroom?" she asked.

"Sure, sure," said Mr. Lyons, waving at the kids to line up for the game. She took the bathroom pass down from its peg on the wall. She'd bet Mr. Lyons wouldn't even remember she'd left, he was so caught up in the dodgeball frenzy. Perfect.

She raced through the first hall as fast as she could without making much noise, creeping up around the corners and watching both ways. *Silly,* she thought, laughing at herself. *You don't need to sneak. You've got a hall pass!* Good thing, too, because the next hall, the long artery that ran from one length of the building to the other, had several teachers in it. B slowed her pace and nodded politely at them.

She slipped into the girls' bathroom, as they would expect her to. She'd wait until they'd walked away. After testing all the taps, she decided it was safe to take a peek. The coast was clear and she was off on soft feet once more until she arrived at Jason's locker. Fourth one to the left of the squirting drinking fountain.

She pulled the latch. Locked, of course. Some kids left theirs ready to reopen easily, but not Jason. That was no surprise. He didn't trust anyone. Sneaks never did.

Magic would help, if she really had any. It was time to test it. She looked both ways to make sure no one was there to watch. What to spell? She wasn't sure. She pointed at Jason's locker, just in case that would help. "O-P-E-N," she said.

With a terrific squeal and a bang, the doors to fifty lockers on either side wrenched open and clanged against the locker frames. Every locker in the hall, except Jason's.

B stared at the open lockers. They looked like gaping mouths, as flabbergasted as she was.

It worked! B caught herself doing her Cauldron Boogie. But only for a millisecond, because astonished voices were drifting out from the classrooms. The noise! B realized, with a panic, that she only had seconds to fix this problem before half a dozen teachers appeared. They'd be sure to ask a few pointed questions about how all the lockers in the hall could suddenly open.

There wasn't time to shut the doors by hand, and there wasn't time to run away. "C-L-O-S-E." She panted, her eyes closed tight.

They closed. All of them. With another huge bang.

B leaped into a narrow recess in the wall next to the drinking fountain. It might not be deep enough to shield her whole body, though. "H-I-D-E," she whispered.

The drinking fountain disappeared. Rats! She squeezed herself tighter into the recess. *I meant hide me*, she thought desperately.

B stood frozen stiff, like a fugitive under a police searchlight.

"Lorraine! What on earth was that?" a teacher called to another.

"I don't know, Earl. Air conditioner trouble, maybe?"

"Sounded like lockers."

"Don't see how it could have been. Everything looks normal."

B could barely keep her breath quiet. Somehow, none of the teachers had seen her. But she felt certain they would hear her breathing, or her heart thumping in her chest.

She had her magic, that was certain. But she was going to need a *lot* more practice!

Chapter 11

B waited a minute more, until the coast was clear. She stepped out of her hiding place and spelled R-E-A-P-P-E-A-R, and the water fountain returned.

Only then did B realize she was trembling. That was a close one.

Her mouth was dry. She bent over the spigot to get a drink from the fountain. And got her face blasted with jet-powered water that went up her nose.

Typical, she thought.

As soon as her face was dry, she sprinted back down the hall. Once outside the gym, she slowed down, walked in nonchalantly, and hung the bathroom pass on the peg by the door.

George's eyebrows rose, asking her how it went. She shook her head and rejoined the dodgeball game, hanging back where George was.

"No, what?" George whispered. "Meaning, no tickets?"

B could hardly hear him over the screech of rubber sneakers on the wood floor. "Meaning, couldn't open Jason's locker." She leaped behind George to avoid a red rubber missile. George, startled, only barely caught the ball, sending Lisa Donahue to the bleachers.

"Does that mean we're stuck?" George asked.

B didn't answer. She wasn't ready to admit that, but she couldn't think of what to do next. While she puzzled over it, an easy throw from Carlos Wilson plastered her in the shoulder. Jason laughed, of course. B shambled over to the bleachers and buried her chin in her hands.

She didn't have a backup plan. If only Jason would just tell the truth . . . Fat chance of that.

Unless, maybe, his honesty got a little magical help.

The phone in Mr. Lyons's office rang, and he blew his whistle. "Take a break, kids," he said, and disappeared to answer it. George came and sat by her.

"George," B whispered, "let's interrogate Jason. Like on detective TV shows. You can be all tough and macho. I'll ask the questions."

"Sure," George said. "Sounds fun, even if there's not a chance he'll tell the truth."

"We might be able to catch him in a lie."

B hid a grin as George puffed out his chest and swaggered toward Jason.

Jason saw them coming and stood up to walk away.

"Hey, Jameson," George growled, his voice much deeper than normal. "We wanna talk wich you."

Jason scowled. "Well, maybe I don't want to talk to *you* and Wasp Brain."

"You usually have plenty to say to me, *Rudolph*," B retorted. "We only want to ask you a question."

"Yeah," George said out of one corner of his mouth, still acting like a mobster. "The lady has some questions for ya, bub. And that's *Miss* Wasp Brain to you."

Jason blinked, not sure what to make of this. B took advantage of this distraction. She glared at Jason and whispered, "T-R-U-T-H!"

"So ask your stupid question, already," Jason said. "Or else buzz off, Hornet."

B cleared her throat. "Did you stay in the class-room after the fire alarm bell rang so that you could save Mozart?"

Jason looked as if he was trying to nod, but his neck had stopped working. His face contorted angrily. "No," he blurted out. He clapped his hand over his mouth.

George glanced at B, forgetting to act tough.

B felt her confidence rise. "Did you steal some-thing today and hide it in your backpack?"

Jason glared at B. His head was starting to twitch. He grabbed his chin and pinned his lips together, as if he wouldn't let them open. Then his head nodded, apparently against his will.

George's jaw dropped open.

"Was it the Black Cats tickets?" she asked.

"No," Jason said, his eyes wide.

B was stunned. No? He hadn't stolen the tickets?

Jason jumped up and pushed past them angrily, climbing higher on the bleachers. George was about to follow, when Mr. Lyons returned from his phone call. He clapped his hands. "C'mon, all-stars, there's time for one more game. Get off the bleachers and line up in teams."

As George and B assumed their places on the gym floor, B's mind reeled. Was it possible that Jason wasn't the thief? That, maybe, he'd stolen someone's lunch money or baseball cards?

Then B remembered Dawn's friends and their beauty spells. Beginner spells didn't last long. Maybe her truth charm had worn off.

"Look sharp there, Jameson," Mr. Lyons called. "I said get off those bleachers and get into the game!"

Jason climbed down as slowly as he could.

"What's the matter, Jason, you afraid to play dodgeball?" Jamal teased.

"Yes!" Jason whimpered, and ran into the locker room.

Now it was B whose jaw dropped. So the truth spell was still working! There was no way Jason the bully would have willingly admitted his fear to the whole class.

Jason didn't come out of the locker room for the rest of gym period, leaving B to play dodgeball in peace. All the while, though, her mind was churning. If Jason didn't steal the tickets, then who did? And what *did* Jason Jameson steal?

Chapter 12

"That was amazing! Jason admitted stealing," George said as they headed down the hall after gym.

"It must have been your accent," B teased.

George grinned. "I'm definitely gonna use that again. But now what? He knows we suspect him so he'll be on his guard around us."

"What we need," B said, "is an eyewitness. Someone who passed the classroom at just the right moment or something."

"I think you're out of luck," George said. "Everyone had left for the fire drill. Your only eyewitness would be Mozart."

"Okay," B said, laughing. "You go to science. I'll just stop in Mr. Bishop's room and interview Mozart."

Wait a minute . . .

If magic could make Jason tell the truth, making a hamster talk might just work! At least, it was worth a try.

"Hey — what did the hamster say when asked why he likes to spin in circles?" George piped up. "Just keeping it wheel. Get it? They spin on those wheels."

George was unstoppable. B felt a little pang for her friend. If her spell worked, George would love a talking hamster. She didn't like keeping this secret from him.

"I forgot my homework," she said. "I'll see you in class." B hurried toward Mr. Bishop's room, hoping he'd be in the faculty lounge, the office, the bathroom, *anywhere* but in his own classroom. Sure enough, when B got there, the room was empty, except for Mozart, who was licking the knob of his slow-drip water bottle. B knew she didn't have much time.

"S-P-E-A-K," she whispered.

Mozart stopped slurping at his drinking tube and started yelling.

"Oh, c'mon, c'mon, why can't you just for once flow, you stupid nozzle, I am so thirsty from running on that wheel I could drink a whole bottle in one gulp but *nooooooo*, you make me lick and lick and lick and lick until my tongue's about worn out, and then there's nothing else to do but run on that wheel. Run, lick, run, lick, eat, sleep, poop. I was born for more than this!"

Suddenly, he turned his attention to B, who was staring at him with her mouth hanging open. "And why can't the great galumphing idiot humans, like *you*, see that? 'Cause you only see what you want to see, you never pay attention to what's really going on right under your nose. And you smaller ones are the worst of the lot. Why did I end up being a middle school hamster and not a retirement home hamster? There's a cushy job, sit on a soft lap once in a while, the old folks pet you real gentle. But *nooooo*, I've got to put up with rotten noisy brats jabbing at me with pencils, like they think I'm a water balloon for them to pop. And banging on my cage! How'd you like it if some giant banged on the walls of your rooms anytime, night or day? Bet you'd be freaked out. Wouldn't you?"

Mozart stamped his tiny foot, which rippled the fur on his belly. He peered up at B angrily, his soft pink nose twitching.

"Holy cats," B said softly to herself. "It worked, and now I'm being chewed out by a hamster!" It was hard to believe this wasn't a daydream. "I'm sorry, Mozart," she said. "I'm really sorry some of the kids make your life so hard."

Mozart picked up a piece of hamster kibble between his front paws and nibbled it. "And this garbage they feed me! I should be eating fresh, tender, succulent grasses. They go down nice and easy. Not like this" — he punted the brown chunk of kibble across his cage — "this *cardboard* you humans buy."

And B thought she had it bad, eating cafeteria food every day at lunch. "I'm sorry about that, too, Mozart."

"Ah, well," he said, "it is what it is, what am I gonna do about it, you know what I mean? Don't go crying your brains out on my account. You're the one who tries to save me from that one nasty kid. The one with all the blotchy things on his face?"

B grinned. "They're freckles," she said, "and that's Jason."

When B spoke Jason's name, Mozart spat out his mouthful. "I don't trust that one," he said. "Not as far as I can throw him."

B giggled, trying to imagine Mozart throwing Jason. But she didn't have time to waste.

"Mozart," she said, "what did Jason do when he stayed in the classroom today? I mean, after the fire drill. You know, the water and loud noises. He told us he stayed to rescue you."

"Me! Rescue me? Are they feeding you bad lettuce? He was messing around over there" — Mozart pointed toward Mr. Bishop's desk — "making noises. *Beep . . . beep! Ch-ch-ch-ch.*"

The teacher's desk was nowhere near the bulletin board where the tickets had been pinned. B had to keep asking questions. Her palms were sweaty with anticipation, not to mention the fear of getting caught talking to a hamster.

"Mozart," B said, using her gentlest voice, "did Jason take the tickets that were pinned to the bulletin board?"

Mozart's paunchy cheeks quivered with chewing. "Trying to get me to tell on your classmate, are ya?" Mozart said, crumbs of kibble falling from his teeth. "I ain't no rat."

B glanced at the clock. Any second now, someone was bound to come in.

"Mozart," she said softly, "this is Jason we're talking about. The blotchy kid who pokes you."

Mozart polished off his kibble and began pawing through his sawdust, fluffing and patting it into a little nest. B was just about to give up.

"Tickets, you say?" Mozart said, through a cloud of sawdust. "Those white things?"

B froze. "That's right," she said, not daring to breathe. The first bell rang for class. *I should go,* B thought. *I'm so close to an answer, though. . . .*

But now Mozart was cozying and burrowing

down into his nest of fluff. He seemed much more interested in a nap.

"Well?" she asked. "Was it Jason who took them?"

Mozart poked up a pink nose. "Nope."

"No?"

Mozart chattered his teeth at her. "I already told you. No."

B clenched and unclenched her fists. Jason had said he hadn't, under the influence of a truth spell. And now Mozart, who certainly had no use for Jason, was backing up his story! B was flummoxed. She picked up her bag and started to turn away.

"If it wasn't Jason who stole the tickets," she thought aloud, "who did?"

Mozart stamped and patted his nest in an ever-quickening frenzy. Wood shavings went flying. Then suddenly, he stopped and stared at her. "You really want to know who made them disappear?"

B looked into his beady little eyes. "Yes!"

He pointed a tiny clawed paw at B.

"You."

Chapter 13

Voices from the hallway snapped B out of her bewilderment. She'd better get out of there.

She darted toward the door.

"That's all right, don't thank me for solving your little mystery," Mozart called. "I get no respect."

Whoops! She couldn't leave Mozart ranting. "S-P-E-E-C-H-L-E-S-S," she hissed, concentrating on the furry creature. Then she ducked her head and scrambled out the door, nearly colliding with a couple of eighth-graders.

For the umpteenth time that day, B sprinted her way silently through the halls, praying at each turn not to get caught. With every step, B's mind reeled from Mozart's revelation.

She stole the tickets?

She, Beatrix, who never stole a thing in her life except gum from Dawn's book bag, and that didn't count since a) she was her sister, and b) Dawn always helped herself to B's licorice?

It was impossible!

Had she been sleepwalking?

Did she have an evil twin?

Did Jason Jameson have a B costume?

No, no, and no. Those were all ridiculous. But so was the thought that she'd taken the Black Cats tickets. She wanted to *earn* them, not steal them.

Could Mozart have confused her with some other girl? Maybe humans looked alike to him?

B remembered the accusation in his voice. For a four-inch rodent, he seemed pretty sure of himself.

While she gathered her science book from her locker, B's thoughts split in a hundred different directions. She hadn't stolen the tickets, and she was pretty sure she wasn't going crazy. But why would Mozart lie? What made him think B was the thief?

She tried to play through all that had happened

in class. She had left the room with everyone else, so it had to be before the fire alarm. But before the alarm, they'd all been practicing spelling.

Spelling!

She'd spelled . . . chaos. That was it. And right after that, the sprinklers and smoke alarms started going crazy.

Could it be that *she* had caused the fire alarm by spelling "chaos"? But chaos shouldn't have made the tickets vanish into thin air.

Vanish.

No, not vanish.

But what about *disguise*?

That was the other word she'd spelled! And she'd been thinking about the tickets when she did it! The tickets must have disguised themselves.

Holy cats! She'd solved the mystery. She could fix this in a snap, and the spelling bee could go on. Competing in the spelling bee would clearly be tricky with her new powers, but B felt sure she could find a way.

B rushed back to her English classroom, which was still empty.

"Thanks, Mozart," she called out on her way to the bulletin board. She reached up and felt the area around the thumbtack. Rough corkboard, and then, smooth paper. She sighed with relief, and said, "R-E-V-E-A-L."

And the tickets shimmered into view.

B couldn't help herself. Once more she stroked the tickets. *I'm gonna win you*, she thought.

"There," she told Mozart. "Problem solved."

"I don't think so," said Mr. Bishop's voice from the doorway.

B froze.

This, she knew, *really* did not look good.

Mr. Bishop approached and leaned against the bulletin board. "I'm glad you returned the tickets, Beatrix," he said. He folded his arms across his chest. "But I'm deeply sorry you took them in the first place."

B's mouth felt as dry as the desert she'd accidentally conjured in the soccer field.

"You made the right choice," Mr. Bishop said. "I will, however, need to speak with your parents about this."

B clamped her eyes shut so the tears welling inside them wouldn't show. It stung terribly to be thought a thief. And there was nothing she could say to disprove it! She couldn't tell him about her magic.

"I must say, Beatrix," Mr. Bishop went on, "I expected better things from you."

B nodded. She couldn't bring herself to face him.

"Is there anything at all you'd like to say to me?" he said, watching her closely.

"Can I go to science now?" she mumbled.

Mr. Bishop sighed. "I guess you'd better."

B's feet carried her the short distance to science class. She sat down at George's table. He stared at her through lab goggles. "What's the matter with you? Need a Mint Fizz?"

B blew her nose. "No, thanks," she said. "Nothing's the matter." She tossed her tissue into the trash. "Listen, it wasn't Jason who stole the tickets."

George's eyebrows rose under his goggles. "How do you know?"

B sighed. "I just know. Anyway, they're back, and the spelling bee can go on now."

"Cool!" George said.

"But . . ."

"Backpacks away, long hair pulled back, goggles on, class!" Mr. Lorry cried, bursting into the room with his lab coat on. "Today we experiment with fire!"

B was glad Mr. Lorry cut her off. How could she explain to George that *she* was the thief?

At the end of the day, B hurried out without waiting for George, grabbed her things from her locker, and headed for the bus.

She had been so excited about getting her magic and solving the mystery of the missing tickets — but both things had turned out to get her into serious trouble. She'd be able to explain to her parents what happened, but she'd still have to take whatever punishment Mr. Bishop gave her, because she couldn't tell him the truth.

But worst of all was George. What was he going to do when he found out, after helping her chase after Jason all day?

What a mess!

Maybe she would get lucky. Maybe Mr. Bishop wouldn't tell the whole school.

All this was enough to make B wish she hadn't gotten her magic.

Chapter 14

George caught the bus the next morning, and, much to B's relief, was his normal, friendly self, telling jokes and giving her chocolate, which meant that Mr. Bishop hadn't told everyone about the tickets yet. But B knew it was just a matter of time.

She hadn't been able to warn her parents, either, because they'd been out at an Enchanted Chocolate Ball until after she'd gone to bed.

B and George trudged into school together, just behind Jason, who pushed past them to walk into school first.

"I wish we could have figured out what he stole," George said.

"You and me both," B said. Then something caught her eye. She held out an arm to stop George from going farther. "What's he doing now?"

Jason had stopped by his locker. He was leaning in, then looking around suspiciously. George and B walked up behind him. Jason had taken a paper from his backpack and was studying it, it seemed, his eyes scanning rapidly through the rows, his lips moving.

"He looks like he's practicing spelling!" B whispered as she and George continued down the hall. "Do you suppose . . ." Her mind whirled back to the strange noises Mozart had made when he described Jason's actions, over by Mr. Bishop's desk. *Beep . . . beep. Ch-ch-ch-ch.* Those were the sounds a printer would make!

She grabbed George's sleeve. "I think Jason stole the word list for the spelling bee!"

George's eyes widened. "Why didn't we think of that before? It's just the kind of thing he'd do!"

"We've got to prove it, or he'll win the bee — and the Black Cats tickets — for sure," B said. "Let's get closer."

But Jason finished his cramming and stuffed the paper back into his bag. He slammed his locker and took off down the hall. What could they do? They couldn't tackle him in front of a hundred students.

B smiled grimly. Being a witch had its advantages. She focused her eyes on his backpack — not easy to do as he darted through the halls. Softly she whispered, "U-N-Z-I-P."

Jason's backpack unzipped and the front flap uncurled like a banana peel. Papers, books, and wadded-up candy wrappers cascaded onto the floor.

George glanced at B, astonished. "What are the chances of that?" he said. "C'mon, let's see what he's got!"

They scurried to where Jason knelt, scrambling to gather his things.

"Let me help you with that, Jameson," George said, picking up Jason's bag. "Oh, geez, looks like every single thing fell out of your backpack. That's a shame!"

"Give me that!" Jason snatched at his bag.

"Here," B said. "These must be your papers. Why,

what's this?" She examined one with interest. "Your older sister's book report on *Charlotte's Web*?"

"None of your beeswax," Jason snapped.

George, standing behind Jason, caught B's eye and waved a folded sheet of paper in the air. He winked. Jason, seeing B look at George, turned to follow her gaze. B grabbed Jason's sleeve to distract him while George stuffed the paper into his pocket.

"Hey, Jason," B said. "Who do you think's gonna win the spelling bee today? Kim? Jenny? Everyone knows they're the smartest kids in our class."

"No, they're not," Jason said. "I got a higher grade on both of the last two book reports than either Kim or Jenny."

"Yeah, but they do better than you on spelling quizzes. And so does George."

From behind Jason's back, George gave B a thumbs-up.

"Well, see you in class," B said. "May the best speller win."

Jason stuffed his papers and books in a crumpled mess back into his bag. "I'm sure he will, Hornet," he said with a sneer. He hurried off.

George grinned at B, pulling the paper out from behind his back. "Got it!" They raced around the corner so they could examine the list. "That was so cool, how his bag came open!" He unfolded the paper. "There it is, the spelling list. 'Grade Six English Spelling Bee List, Draft One,'" he read.

"Don't read the words," B said. "We're not cheats like Jason. But now we've got the proof, and we can take it to Mr. Bishop. . . ." B's smile faded. "Oh, no!" She felt sick to her stomach.

"What's the matter?"

B crumpled the paper into a ball. "We don't have proof that Jason stole the list," she said. "What we have is proof that *we* did."

Chapter 15

George took the paper wad from B's hand, shaking his head. "All that effort for nothing." He found a trash can and, when no one was watching, buried the list deep inside.

"It's not completely wasted," B said. "*We* know he stole the list. If he does win, at least we'll know the truth. That's worth something."

George snapped his fingers. "I've got an idea! You could tell Mr. Bishop that you . . . heard a rumor, or something, about Jason stealing the list. After all, he admitted that he stole something." George paused. "And I'm telling you: Jason stole it! There, the rumor's started."

B's shoulders sagged. "I don't think I want to tell Mr. Bishop that," she said. "I'm . . . not sure that he'll believe me."

"Why wouldn't he?"

B looked away. "Oh, I dunno." She saw, from the concerned look on his face, that he was going to ask another question, so she headed him off. "Got any more of those Enchantomallow Cremes?"

George handed her the entire bag. "To tide you over until English," he said. B took the bag with a half smile.

She headed for homeroom. She sat through morning announcements with a gnawing feeling in her stomach. She'd solved all the puzzles but it didn't matter; Jason got off scot-free, and Mr. Bishop thought she was a thief.

She'd discovered her magic, but it was a weird, unpredictable kind, and one that was bound to trip her up in the spelling bee.

Who knew what might happen when she spelled words aloud? Maybe she'd turn Jason into a toad. That would be some consolation.

When third period rolled around, B shuffled into Mr. Bishop's room and took her seat in time to hear Jason bragging to Jenny about winning the bee. B couldn't bear it. She glanced over to see Mozart standing in the front corner of his cage, scratching at the glass, his soft white belly pressed against it. It almost seemed as if he was waving at her. She waved back and made a mental note to bring in some freshly picked grass tomorrow.

"As you can see, class, the tickets have returned," Mr. Bishop said the moment the bell had rung. "It must have been magic."

B gulped. If only he knew! But she was grateful he hadn't told the class *who* brought them back.

Mr. Bishop went on, waving his list in the air. "Now it's time to start. Line up in front. Did everyone study? Eat a good breakfast? Ready to show us what you can do with words?" His eyes met B's as he spoke. He'd never believe it if he knew. . . .

They lined up in the front of the room. B frowned at the paper in Mr. Bishop's hands. Another printout of the spelling list. Out of the corner of her eye, she saw Jason eyeing it, too, struggling to suppress a cocky grin.

Darn that Jason! B refused to give up. What good was magic if she couldn't . . .

Holy cats! Why didn't she think of it sooner?

There *was* something B could do.

"C-H-A-N-G-E," she whispered, staring at the paper and praying that it wouldn't change into a walrus.

The paper remained a paper. Mr. Bishop watched her, the tip of his beard twitching. Maybe he'd over-heard her spelling and thought she was practicing for the competition.

He looked back at the paper, blinked, and scratched his head. "This is strange," he said. "I seem to have printed the wrong spelling list." He glanced at B, then back at the list. "Never mind. These words will do just fine."

"Uh . . . we can wait, Mr. Bishop," Jason said. "Why don't you go ahead and find the first draft? We're not going anywhere."

George leaned forward and turned to see B, his eyebrows wagging. Of course, he couldn't know B had changed the list magically, but he knew this was bad news for Jason!

Mr. Bishop waved Jason silent. "The first draft, eh?" he said. "No, I like this list just fine." He nodded, reading through it silently. "*Extremely* tricky words. This will be a lively competition."

Jason slumped back in his chair.

B pressed her lips tight so the laughter she felt bubbling inside her wouldn't spill out. She'd done it! She'd saved the spelling bee. She nearly burst into her happy dance. What was better than seeing Jason get what he deserved? Not much!

"Well, let's get started. George, your word is 'deceitful.'"

George sailed smoothly through, remembering the "i before e, except after c" rule. Other kids' turns followed, and Jason, B was pleased to see, seemed more nervous than anyone else. He managed his first word, "festering," without any trouble.

Then it was B's turn. She held her breath. Would she be able to spell the word? She wasn't afraid of not knowing the spelling . . . she was terrified of causing more mayhem.

"Business," Mr. Bishop said.

"Business," B repeated. Well, what harm could that do? She tried to empty her mind so that nothing could be influenced by her word. But emptying one's mind is about as easy as not thinking of flaming salamanders when someone tells you not to think of flaming salamanders. So instead, she tried to think of her dad's sales figures at Enchanted Chocolates Worldwide.

"You still with us, B?" Mr. Bishop said.

"Sorry," B said. "Business. B-U-S-I-N-E-S-S. Business."

She looked around the room. Nothing changed. No sirens approached, no tickets vanished, and there were no screams from the soccer field.

"That's right," Mr. Bishop said.

B nodded, smiling. So far, so good. She just hoped business would be good for Dad today.

They went around the class. Jimmy misspelled "embarrass," and Claudia put an extra "s" in "disease" — B was grateful she hadn't gotten that word — but otherwise everyone spelled their words right. George aced "fidelity," and Jason managed "fiend" (like "friend," without the "r," that was B's trick for it). Soon it was B's turn again.

"Explosion," Mr. Bishop said.

Oh, no!

Mr. Bishop watched her. His beard twitched.

B searched around the room for anything that could explode harmlessly. A squooshy stress-reliever ball on the teacher's desk? Too risky. Even exploding marshmallows could be dangerous. And what if her magic didn't work right?

"Explosion," B whispered, her mouth dry as salt. "Um, E . . . X . . . P . . ."

She became conscious of all the other eyes in the room, staring at her. *I have to misspell it,* she thought miserably. *There's no other way. Bye-bye, tickets.*

"B, are you all right?" Mr. Bishop asked.

She bit her lip and nodded.

"Why don't you start the word again?"

"E-X-P-L-O . . . ," She paused, and sighed. "S-O-N."

Jason Jameson snorted with laughter. George elbowed him.

Mr. Bishop lowered his paper. "I'm sorry, B, that's incorrect."

B met George's gaze as she headed for her seat. If he was surprised she had missed such an easy word, he didn't show it. She smiled to thank him. More than anything, she wished she could explain to George why she'd misspelled her word.

"Mr. Bishop," Jason whined, "George hit me!"

Mr. Bishop glanced over the top of his paper. "Kim, you're next, and your word is 'rivalry.'"

Kim spelled the word correctly, and the competition went on. Several students stumbled during this round, which was some comfort — B wasn't the only one to fall. Colby tripped on "mediocre," Travis collapsed under "onslaught," and Michaela flubbed "vacuum." Even Jamal botched "asparagus," adding an extra "u" in the middle.

Jason's turn came around again. Mr. Bishop, B was sure, had a slightly evil gleam in his eye. "Surreptitious," he said.

Jason looked like a soldier facing a firing squad. He thrust his lower lip out in a pout. "Mr. Bishop, these are really hard! We've never studied words like these before."

"Oh?" Mr. Bishop said. "Does anyone here know what 'surreptitious' means?"

To her surprise, B found herself raising her hand.

"Yes, B?"

"It means sneaky," B said, glaring at Jason. "Doing things on the sly so no one will know."

Mr. Bishop nodded. "That's right." He paused, then pointed a finger at Jason. "Now, Mr. Jameson, will you please spell 'surreptitious'?"

Jason swallowed. "Surreptitious," he said, with a squeak in his voice. "Um, S-Y-R-U-P-T-I-C-I-O-U-S?"

B wanted to gloat, but she wasn't about to stoop as low as Jason, so she folded her hands on her desk and studied Mozart like she'd never seen him before. He paused from licking his watering tube to wave a paw at her.

"I'm sorry, Jason. That's not correct."

Thwarting Jason the Sneak was a fabulous feeling. Almost as thrilling as winning the Black Cats tickets might have been. She gave George her best good-luck grin.

The contest went on. Soon it came down to a threesome of Jenny, George, and Kim, dueling like spelling swordfighters. Soon Jenny succumbed to "sanctimonious," a word that drew gasps from the rest of the room.

Then George and Kim faced off. They went through three more rounds, and then Kim was handed "cemetery."

Overconfidence was her downfall. "C-E-M-E-T-A-R-Y," she spelled quickly.

Mr. Bishop shook his head. "I'm sorry, Kim." He looked at George. "Young man, if you can spell this next word correctly, you are the class champion, and the Black Cats tickets are yours. Are you ready?"

George nodded. B gripped the edge of her desk so hard, her knuckles turned white.

"Your word is 'conjurer.'"

B laughed quietly. She knew that one.

"Conjurer," George said. "C-O-N-J-U-R-E-R."

Mr. Bishop tossed his spelling list high in the air. "The winner!" And the whole class, or rather, *almost* the whole class, jumped up and cheered for George. Even Kim. B rushed over to hug her friend. Out of the corner of her eye, she saw the spelling list drift down through the air like a feather and land on Jason's desk. Jason tore it in two.

"You did it!" she told George. "You won the tickets!"

Other kids swarmed around George, patting his back and congratulating him. B smiled. Everything had worked out! Mr. Bishop hadn't mentioned B in connection with the returned tickets. Jason the Sneak had lost, and her best friend had won. She was so proud of him.

Mr. Bishop handed the tickets to George just as the bell rang. Everyone grabbed their things and headed for the door, talking loudly about the competition and groaning about the words they'd missed. In the middle of the commotion, George slipped something into B's hand.

It was a Black Cats ticket.

She didn't know what to say, except, "Holy cats!"

Her cheering froze when she felt a heavy hand on her shoulder. This sinking feeling was getting all too familiar.

"B," Mr. Bishop said. "May I see you for a moment?"

Chapter 16

George was puzzled, but he didn't pry. "I'll see you at lunch," he said, leaving B alone in the classroom with Mr. Bishop. But Mr. Bishop called after George, "Young man! Just so you know, B may not be able to join you at lunch today. We have a lot of work to do."

B sat down in an empty desk and stared at its smudgy surface, her cheeks burning, waiting for whatever lecture or interrogation Mr. Bishop had in mind. Was he going to send her to detention for stealing the tickets? She still clutched her ticket in her sweaty palm, wondering if the teacher was going to take it away, since she was the supposed thief. Or maybe he would decide she would have to tell everyone what she'd done. . . .

Mr. Bishop bent down and picked up the torn halves of the spelling list from where Jason had dropped them. He sat in the desk in front of B and twisted around to face her.

"Beatrix," he said. Uh-oh, Beatrix again. "Did you misspell 'explosion' on purpose?"

B looked up, startled. How did he know? Helpless, she nodded.

"Why?"

B kept her eyes lowered. "I get scared of speaking in front of people," she said. That part was true, at least.

"Yes, but to intentionally misspell a word that you know misrepresents your capabilities," Mr. Bishop said. "It's a form of dishonesty to let the world think you're not as bright as you really are."

B didn't know what to think. Was Mr. Bishop trying to encourage her to have more self-confidence, or was he about to call her parents to report *today's* act of dishonesty? B suddenly felt tired. She wished Mr. Bell had never bought that lottery ticket, and that none of this drama had ever begun.

Mr. Bishop indicated to the spelling list fragments. "Funny how this list changed into harder words, right before my eyes . . ." he said. Panic rose up in B's stomach. "You know what I think, B?"

She couldn't even imagine how he could explain magically appearing words. All she was sure of was that it would probably spell T-R-O-U-B-L-E. "What?"

"I think words are like birds; they flutter and flit. Use them wisely and who knows what might come of it?"

B cocked her head to one side. What a weird thing to say! It almost sounded like one of her mother's couplets.

Then she realized that the words on the torn-up spelling list were leaping, one by one, into the air, like a flock of birds taking flight from a tree branch. They spun and twirled around B's head, then popped, making twinkly sounds.

B stared at Mr. Bishop. The corners of his mouth twitched.

"You're . . . you're . . ."

"That's right," he said, grinning. "I'm a witch. Just like you."

B rubbed her eyes and stared again at the blank paper where the spelling words had been. "But how did you know that I . . . Who told you . . ."

Mr. Bishop folded his hands behind his head. "I'm from the Magical Rhyming Society, B. I'm in charge of the Developmental Magical Inquiry Committee. I was sent to observe you, to try to discover why you hadn't found your magical powers yet."

B shook her head. "The Magical Rhyming Society was worried about *me*?"

Mr. Bishop nodded. "Waiting for magic to emerge is hard on anyone. We all remember what it was like. In my department, I study different kinds of magic. You, B, have an extraordinary gift — a rare and powerful form of magic."

B felt like she was wading through molasses, just

trying to keep up with this information. "You mean . . . Mr. Bell didn't win the lottery?" she said.

Mr. Bishop laughed. "He did win. But, it may not have been entirely by chance." He winked. "I suspect he misses you kids, and when he's done loafing around on a Hawaiian beach, he may even want his job back. Not right away, though. I'm enjoying myself here. And it's clear that the average sixth-grader in this town has a lot to learn about the power of words. I think I'll stick around."

"Good." B smiled. And, she realized, she meant it. She always knew there was something she liked about Mr. Bishop, even when he was hard on her. This explained everything.

Almost everything.

"I didn't steal the tickets, you know," she said, relieved that she could finally set the record straight. "I was thinking about them when I spelled the word 'disguise.'"

Mr. Bishop threw back his head and laughed. "I should have known! My biggest clue about your spelling magic was the chaos you'd caused. But I never made the connection with 'disguise.' You must have figured it out yesterday, when I caught you in the room with the tickets."

"I had a little help," B said. She looked over at Mozart. "S-P-E-A-K."

"Well, it's about time you two knuckleheads figured this out," Mozart squeaked. "I've been trying to tell both of you: She's a witch, and he's a witch, and nobody took the tickets, she just hid 'em is all, and I've been squeaking myself hoarse over here, and does anybody pay any attention to the hamster? *Nooo*, you just go on being dunderheads, having your spelling bees and blaming the wrong people left and right. Every time that girl got up to spell, I had to burrow deep in my sawdust for protection. No telling what might happen! And you! Big guy there, who should have known better, giving her the word 'explosion'? Next time, just bring a stick of dynamite into the classroom. That's what that girl is. Dynamite."

"Enough!" Mr. Bishop clapped his hands over his ears. "I agree with you, Mozart, but enough already."

"Sorry, Mozart," B said. "S-P-E-E-C-H-L-E-S-S." And Mozart went back to softly cheeping in hamster-talk.

"I was sure you were going to tell everyone I was the thief," B continued.

"I just had a feeling that I should hold out," Mr. Bishop said. "I was right, B. Your magic is powerful indeed. There are very few witches alive today who can do things like make animals talk. And your spells last awhile, don't they?" He laughed. "The firemen had a terrible time getting the alarm system turned off. And Coach Lyons is still growling about the athletic field being covered in sand. . . . Did you have a hand in that, I wonder?"

B felt guilty again, but Mr. Bishop put his hand on her shoulder and spoke a rhyme.

"B's power is sure to bring her notoriety.
Bring her now to the Magical Rhyming Society!"

A strong wind rushed around her and Mr. Bishop. The room seemed to spin and blur, and in a moment they were transported to the most enormous library B had ever seen — a circular room several stories high, with bookshelves lining every wall, and hundreds of magicians in glittering robes climbing the ladders and walkways to reach the books. The whole room positively hummed with rhymes. Whorls of sparkling light and showers of twinkling stars danced in the air with every spell cast. A wonderful fragrance, like berries in spring, and summer roses, filled the air.

"Welcome, B, to the Magical Rhyming Society," Mr. Bishop said. "Only witches who have found their magic are able to enter. And here you are at last!"

Chapter 17

"Doug! Oh, Doug!" a shrill voice cried.

"Right here," Mr. Bishop called, waving to a tall, skinny witch who was rapidly climbing down a ladder from the bookshelves in the topmost tower.

The tall witch slid, fireman-style, down the last few flights of the library, and raced to join them where they stood in the center of the room.

"Is this she?" the witch demanded, peering at B through purple crescent-moon-shaped spectacles. "Is this the spelling prodigy you told me about?"

"This is Beatrix," Mr. Bishop said. "B, to her friends. And yes, she's every bit as extraordinary as I told you. Even more so."

B blushed to hear this praise, but her attention

was riveted by the extraordinary lady who stood before her.

She wasn't just tall; she was *extremely* tall, and beanpole thin. Her hair wasn't white, as B had first thought, but baby blue, and twisted into an elegant bun. Behind her purple spectacles, sparkling black eyes gave B the impression that she could read B as easily as she might read a book on one of these shelves. Her robe was woven of blue, green, and silver threads, and was so spangled with shiny silver charms that she looked like a beautiful coin collection. The charms on her robe tinkled when she moved.

"Well, Doug, aren't you going to introduce me?"

"Sorry," Mr. Bishop said. "B, this is Madame Mellifluous, Grande Mistress of the Magical Rhyming Society and Head Librarian of the society's spell collection."

Madame Mellifluous thrust out a bony hand for B to shake. "Call me Mel," she said. "Mellifluous is a mouthful."

"I can spell it," B said quickly, then wished she hadn't bragged.

Madame Mellifluous smiled. "I'll bet you can." She raised her arms high in the air, and clapped her hands loudly. Her wrists dripped with bracelets, from which hung even more charms.

"Everyone!" she cried. "Come and see our amazing new witch, whose powers are as strong as they are unusual."

Witches in sparkling clothes swarmed across the landings and down the stairs to gather around Madame Mel.

And to stare in wonder at B.

"Um, Mr. Bishop?" B whispered. "Don't I need to get back for gym class now?"

"Gym can wait," he said.

"Send Coach Lyons a tardy slip.

B's here on an important trip."

And right before B's eyes, a pink tardy slip appeared with Mr. Bishop's handwriting on it. It folded itself into a tiny paper airplane and zoomed out a circular window.

"There," her teacher said. "You're off the hook."

But B's attention was already elsewhere. Other witches were starting to appear, as if from nowhere, in glittering cyclones of magical wind. B recognized Macey and Stef, and several witching families she knew, and then her own parents appeared with Dawn. Would they be mad that she hadn't told them first? Her parents' shining faces soon set B's mind at ease. B's mom was hugging onto Dad's arm and dabbing her eyes with a handkerchief.

"Gentlewitches everywhere," Mr. Bishop said, in a booming voice, "it's my pleasure to present to you a young lady whom I know we'll all be hearing more about in the years to come. As you know, my department studies any unusual happenings with magic, and something that hasn't been seen in four generations at least is spelling magic, the kind that is produced when a rare kind of witch spells words. And here before me is Beatrix, known to friends and family as simply 'B,' the first to be born in over a hundred years with that rare and powerful gift."

A gasp of oohs and aahs rippled across the sea of faces. B jammed her hands into her pockets so people wouldn't see them shaking. Were her knees knocking together, or was the whole building trembling?

"B's amazing powers distill the essence of her magic into single words — in fact, into the mere letters that make up those words. She needs no rhyming couplets to produce spells — they don't even work for her. Her magic is powerfully focused, and unlike most young people's spells, hers have staying power."

Some of the mothers in the room gasped as if this was horrifying news. B turned anxiously and saw the long, pointed face of Madame Mel give her a reassuring wink.

"B," Mr. Bishop said eagerly, and, B realized with surprise, a bit nervously, "would you give the society a demonstration?"

The room grew silent. B felt the weight of all those eyes staring at her. She felt like a lump of clay on the table in art class, getting flattened by all the pressure.

B stared down at her sneakers. *I can't do it*, she thought. *I'll mess up big time and . . . set all the books on fire or something. Make them all overdue.*

"Ahem."

Madame Mel was peering at her, a pointy silver boot toe tapping impatiently on the ground. "We're ready," Madame Mel said under her breath.

Maybe B could think of herself and spell E-S-C-A-P-E?

Suddenly, Dawn was climbing up the steps to where B stood. B couldn't bear to face her, but then she felt Dawn slip her arm around her.

"Don't be scared, B," Dawn said.

B grinned, but her eyes grew wet.

"I just want to be a normal witch," she whispered to Dawn. "You know, a rhyming one."

Dawn gave her shoulder a little shake. "Why would you want to be boring old 'normal'?" she said. "You're special! You've got something no one else has."

B sniffled. "What?"

"Me as a big sister." Dawn flashed her movie-star smile. "Go get 'em, B," she said. "Just start with something simple."

"Okay." Having Dawn stand beside her gave her new courage. But still, all those bright lights, all those big eyes staring at her . . . if only she could make them go away.

"D-A-R-K-N-E-S-S," she said.

Instantly, blinds fell over all the windows, and one by one, the globe lightbulbs illuminating the room popped. The room went dark as falling shards of broken glass tinkled. Many witches in the crowd cried out in fear.

Madame Mel's voice cracked out like lightning.

"Protect the kids, the gals and fellas,
Give them all brand-new umbrellas!"

And before the broken glass could land and hurt anyone, B felt a handle in her hand and heard the soft *plip, plip* of fragments landing on the umbrella cloth.

Murmurs and whispers filled the darkness.

B was terrified. Was she going to be in trouble? No way would her allowance cover the cost of so many lights.

"Thank you, B," Madame Mel's voice said, with just enough of an edge that B wasn't sure if she was mad or not. "Would you care to reverse the problem?"

Dawn squeezed her arm reassuringly.

"Okay," B said, her voice faltering. "L-I-G-H-T."

Miniature suns flared into life, hovering in the air above the rainbow of umbrellas.

A single clap rang out. Then another, and soon the entire assembly was applauding her boisterously. Someone shouted, "Bravo!" Everyone folded their umbrellas and put them away. B's mom and dad beamed so warmly at her that B knew she wasn't in trouble. Not at all.

Mr. Bishop held out a sparkling silver chain. "May I see your hand, please?"

B held out her hand, and Mr. Bishop fastened the bracelet around her wrist. "Your magical training has officially begun, B," he said. "Your first spell as a newly inaugurated member of our society will be to create the charm that best represents your own special flavor of magic. Are you ready?"

B admired the intricate chain. It was just like Dawn's, but without the charms. "How will I know what to make?" she asked.

"Don't worry," Dawn said. "Just let it be what it wants to be."

"Everyone, let's give B a hand," Mr. Bishop said, addressing the crowd. "On my signal, spell the word 'charm' along with B. Ready?"

He nodded to B, and she opened her mouth.

"C-H —" It was an amazing feeling, all that witching power in one room, chanting in unison. "— A-R-M."

Something tickled her wrist.

She opened her eyes to a sea of smiling, welcoming faces, and on her wrist, a glittering, silver letter "B."

She held the dangling charm up before her eyes. It shimmered with light from B's magic suns.

"Holy cats!" she whispered. "It's official now, isn't it?"

"Sure is," Dawn said.

Then B was clobbered by a huge hug from her whole family.

B's charmed adventures continue in

Spelling B

And the Trouble with Secrets

By Lexi Connor

SCHOLASTIC

Read on for a sneak peek!

B's alarm clock went off for the third time.

"Q-U-I-E-T," she groaned. The alarm magically stopped — B was grateful again that she'd finally discovered how her magic worked.

B buried her head under a pillow. She'd stayed up way too late last night reading, and she wasn't ready to face the sunshine just yet. Besides, it was only 7:10.

7:10!

7:10 was *not* good. She had only ten minutes to catch the bus and she was still in her pajamas!

She skidded into the bathroom, brushed her teeth, and combed her hair. Two minutes.

Back in her bedroom, she yanked open her drawers and tore through the piles of clothes for something to wear. Black Cats sweatshirt? Her favorite band. Always good. Purple jeans? Sure. Socks? She pulled out one pink and one green. No time to dig for mates. "M-A-T-C-H," she said. They both turned green with pink polka dots. She yanked them on.

She stuck a headband in her hair, fastened her magical charm bracelet — the one she got when she discovered her spelling magic — and glanced at the clock. 7:16. Six minutes down, four to go. If only she could slow down time, she might be able to eat and make the bus. But slowing down time was advanced magic, and she hadn't even had her first magic lesson yet.

If she missed the bus, no magic would avoid Mom and Dad's irritation. She threw her backpack over one shoulder and laced her sneakers.

Sneakers. Feet. She couldn't slow time, but she could speed herself up!

"F-A-S-T," she told her feet. They leaped up and sped down the stairs. Her sneakers were a sparkly blur.

Into the kitchen she zoomed, snagging the warm banana hazelnut muffin hovering over her mother's outstretched hand. Her feet dragged her, knees pumping crazily, to the front door. "Bye!" she cried, her feet still churning. By the time she stuffed a bite of muffin in her mouth, B was halfway to the bus stop on the corner.

Holy cats, my magic is awesome! B thought. *I can sleep in every morning from now on.*

Tails of enchantment!

Read about a very special pet shop—
one where all the animals are magic!

But between one blink and the next, the bus stop was 30 yards behind her.

"Whoa!" she cried. "Slow! Stop! I mean, S-T-O-P!"

B's feet planted themselves in the ground like cement posts. She fell face-forward, *ker-splat*, on the Peabodys' front lawn, smashing her muffin to smithereens.

The school bus pulled around the corner.

"Isn't that your bus coming, Beatrix?" Mrs. Peabody said, coming out onto the porch in a bathrobe and slippers. "What are you doing way over here?"

"S-sorry, Mrs. Peabody," B stammered. "I, uh, got, um, carried away! Bye!" And she raced, normal-style, to the bus stop.

B climbed the bus steps, promising herself she'd be more careful next time. Problem was, all B had to do was spell a word. Pretty quick and easy to do — and therefore, easy to get into trouble.